D1111097

RANGER in TIME

Night of Soldiers and Spies

THE RANGER IN TIME SERIES

RANGER in TIME

Night of Soldiers and Spies

KATE MESSNER

illustrated by
KELLEY McMORRIS

Scholastic Inc.

Text copyright © 2019 by Kate Messner
Illustrations by Kelley McMorris, copyright © 2019 Scholastic Inc.
Photo ©: 127 bottom: Gift of John Stewart Kennedy, 1897/The Metropolitan Museum of Art.

This book is being published simultaneously in hardcover by Scholastic Press.

Library of Congress Cataloging-in-Publication Data
Names: Messner, Kate, author. | McMorris, Kelley, illustrator.
Title: Night of soldiers and spies / Kate Messner ; illustrated by Kelley McMorris.
Description: New York, NY : Scholastic Inc., 2019. | Series: Ranger in time | Summary: Ranger the time-travelling Golden retriever and young Isaac Pope come together in 1776 during Washington's retreat after the Battle of Long Island, and stays with him while he slowly recovers from Smallpox — but Ranger's real mission comes later when Isaac is sent to spy out the Hessian troops' intentions before the Battle of Trenton.
Identifiers: LCCN 2018038977 (print) | LCCN 2018040781 (ebook) |
ISBN 9781338134032 (Ebook) | ISBN 9781338134018 (pbk.) |
ISBN 9781338134025 (jacketed library binding)
Subjects: LCSH: Golden retriever — Juvenile fiction. | Time travel — Juvenile fiction. | Soldiers — Juvenile fiction. | Smallpox — Juvenile fiction. | Espionage, American — Juvenile literature. | Long Island, Battle of, New York, N.Y., 1776 — Juvenile fiction. | Trenton, Battle of, Trenton, N.J., 1776 — Juvenile fiction. | Adventure stories. | United States — History — Revolution, 1775-1783 — Juvenile fiction. | CYAC: Golden retriever — Fiction. | Dogs — Fiction. | Time travel — Fiction. | Smallpox — Fiction. | Spies — Fiction. | Adventure and adventurers — Fiction. | Long Island, Battle of, New York, N.Y., 1776 — Fiction. | Trenton, Battle of, Trenton, N.J., 1776 — Fiction. | United States — History — Revolution, 1775-1783 — Fiction. | GSAFD: Adventure fiction. | LCGFT: Historical fiction. | Action and adventure fiction.
Classification: LCC PZ10.3.M5635 (ebook) | LCC PZ10.3.M5635 Ni 2019 (print) |
DDC 813.6 [Fic] — dc23
LC record available at https://lccn.loc.gov/2018038977

ISBN 978-1-338-13401-8

10 9 8 7 6 5 4 3 2 1   19 20 21 22 23

Printed in the United States of America   40
First printing 2019

Book design by Ellen Duda and Shivana Sookdeo

*For Mrs. Abernathy's classes at
Lucy T. Davis Elementary*

Chapter 1

NO LIGHTS, NO SOUND

Isaac Pope held the flat-bottomed boat steady while soldiers waded into the river and loaded supplies.

"Quickly!" an officer whispered through the pounding rain. "We must have every man across before dawn!"

Isaac nodded but didn't answer aloud. No lights. No sound. That was the order. This mission had to be silent and secret. Anything else would mean disaster.

The boat sank lower in the water until Isaac signaled that it was full. He and the other sailors of the Fourteenth Continental Regiment used poles to push off from shore. It was their second trip of the night.

Their task felt impossible: Ferry nine thousand troops across the mile-long stretch of river between Long Island and New York. Horses and supplies had to be moved, too. All before the sun came up and British troops realized the American Rebels were fleeing. Anyone left behind would be taken prisoner.

For two days, General George Washington's Continental Army had battled British soldiers in the rain. But then the Rebels found themselves surrounded. All day, British troops had ventured closer, digging ditches so they could advance without being exposed to gunfire. In another day, they'd be within musket range, and Washington's army would have to surrender. The revolution would be over almost as

soon as it began. Crossing the East River in darkness was their only hope.

Isaac pulled harder on his oar. His head had been pounding all day. His muscles were aching even before he'd started rowing. Now they burned with every stroke.

But if anyone could get this job done, it was the men of the Fourteenth Continental Regiment. Most had been sailors and fishermen together in Marblehead, Massachusetts, before they signed up for the Continental Army. When the British had closed the Grand Banks to fishing, Isaac and the other men were furious. How would they provide for their families? That was when many of Marblehead's fishermen made the decision to join the Patriot cause and fight for independence from Great Britain.

The commander of their regiment was Colonel John Glover, who took pride in his fishermen's determination and bravery. They had faced long journeys at sea together. They had weathered the wild storms of the Grand Banks. Now General Washington was trusting them with his entire army.

When the New York shore was near and the water shallow enough, the soldiers piled out. Isaac shivered and headed back for another trip. His whole body shook with chills. He was weak with hunger. The driving rain and wind had made it nearly impossible to light fires for cooking. He'd eaten nothing but raw pork and rock-hard biscuits for two days. And there were still so many troops to move.

When Isaac's boat made it back to Brooklyn Heights, the men were fretting and whispering. One of the soldiers leaned in to him. "The tide's turning," he hissed. "Between that and the wind, we can't navigate the sloops anymore. We won't make it."

Isaac looked at his flat-bottomed boat, already filling with anxious men. Without the larger sloops helping to move men, they'd never get everyone across the river before dawn.

Isaac felt dizzy. He imagined the Redcoats waking at first light to find hundreds of Continental soldiers trapped in Brooklyn. Isaac's ears still rang from the gunfire of the day before. He had crouched behind a stone wall, his heart pounding against the musket he'd held tight to his chest.

They'd fought bravely, but how long could they go on? George Washington's troops were beaten down. They'd held out for two days against an army twice their size. But now they were surrounded.

Could they possibly escape before dawn?

Chapter 2

POP! BOOM! BANG!

"Happy Fourth of July, Ranger!" Luke said. "I saved the last piece of my hot dog for you." He leaned down and fed it to Ranger under the picnic table.

Ranger was just finishing when he saw a flash of brown out of the corner of his eye.

Squirrel!

Ranger darted out from under the table and chased the squirrel all around the yard. He chased it past Mom's garden, up the porch steps, and down again. When the squirrel climbed a tree, Ranger sat at the bottom, barking.

"Got outrun again, Ranger," Sadie said, and bent down to pat his head.

That was all right. Ranger didn't know what he'd do if he ever caught a squirrel anyway. He just liked chasing them. Squirrels were the reason Ranger wasn't an official search-and-rescue dog.

Ranger had done all kinds of training with Luke and Dad. He'd practiced finding Luke in the woods and in big warehouses with boxes all over. He'd even practiced finding him when Luke was buried in the snow. Ranger was very good at finding people.

But to be an official search-and-rescue dog, you had to pass a test. And to pass the test, you had to ignore everything except your job. You had to ignore cats and crowds of people and juicy hot dogs dropped in front of you. You even had to ignore squirrels.

On the day of Ranger's test, a squirrel had run right out in front of him. Ranger chased it, even though Dad said no. Ranger knew Luke wasn't really lost. He was just pretending. If a real person had needed help, Ranger would have left the squirrel alone. But that didn't matter. He didn't pass his test, so he didn't get to be a search-and-rescue dog. Now he could chase as many squirrels as he liked.

"Finish up and let's clear the table," Mom said. "We should get Ranger inside before the fireworks start."

Ranger loved Fourth of July hot dogs, but he didn't like the fireworks one bit. They hurt his ears. He always hid under the blanket in his dog bed until the popping and booming ended.

Ranger followed Luke and Sadie inside. He stayed in the mudroom while they went to the kitchen to get marshmallows. As soon as they left, Ranger heard a soft humming sound coming from his bed.

Ranger pawed at his blanket until he uncovered the old first aid kit he'd dug up from the garden one day. The humming was louder now.

Ranger had heard that sound before. The old metal box only hummed when someone far away needed Ranger's help. Once, it had taken him to a giant ship that was about to sink in a frigid sea. Another time, it had taken him to a dusty prairie where a boy and his family were starting out on a dangerous journey. And once, it had taken him to a city shaken by an earthquake, where a girl and her friend were running from fires.

Now the first aid kit was humming again. Ranger lowered his head and nuzzled the strap over his neck. The humming got louder. Light spilled from the cracks in the old metal box. It grew brighter and brighter. Too bright!

Ranger had to close his eyes. He felt as if he were being squeezed through a hole in the sky.

Suddenly, the humming stopped. Ranger opened his eyes.

It was half-dark out, just like it had been at home. But a cool rain had replaced the warm summer weather. Fog and whispers floated through the air as men ran quietly toward a riverbank.

"Hush now, and hurry," one of them ordered. "We're running out of time!"

Chapter 3

LAST CHANCE TO CROSS

Ranger padded through the mud to the edge of the river, where a boy a little older than Luke was holding a boat. One by one, a line of tired-looking men climbed in. The boy's trousers were torn. His coat was streaked with mud. He smelled of smoke, river water, and sweat.

"Sun's starting to rise," Isaac whispered to his friend Joe. Isaac knew Joe from the church back home in Marblehead. Joe was enslaved by a merchant who'd sent him to fight instead of joining the army himself.

Joe nodded. "Don't quit on me now," he

whispered. "You put in longer days than this in the Grand Banks, my friend. How many cod tongues did you say you turned in that day? Two hundred?"

Isaac smiled, even though he trembled with chills. "Two hundred twenty." He still remembered pulling in fish after fish on his hand line that day. The fishermen cut out the tongue of each cod before salting it and tossing it into the hold. At the end of the day, they'd bring all the tongues to an officer to claim credit for their catch. That evening, Isaac had more than anyone.

He had told Joe about his amazing catch when he returned from sea. But somehow it was a better story when Joe told it later that night at the blacksmith's shop. When Joe told a story, all the men put down their drinks to listen. Even if they'd been there, they wanted to hear him tell it.

Isaac looked up the bank, where more men were streaming toward them in the dark. What a story Joe would have to tell of this night.

But before the men arrived, a shaggy, golden dog crept up to the boat.

"What's this?" Joe asked. "One of the general's dogs?"

"Probably." Isaac patted Ranger's head. "You'll have to wait to cross the river, dog. We have more men to move."

"We better hope this fog doesn't lift," Joe said. "It's the only thing hiding our rear guard from the King's troops."

Isaac shivered. He didn't know if it was because of the damp air, his fever, or his fear. He reached into his pocket and squeezed his good-luck charm. It was just a short length of knotted rope, but its rough, scratchy feel always reminded him of home. Isaac's father

had been a mariner, too. When Isaac was a small boy, his father had given him the rope to practice the knots he'd need to know to join the fleet one day.

Isaac had just perfected his bowline knot the summer his father was lost at sea. Isaac never got to show him, and he never untied it. He kept the rope in his pocket, a way of keeping his father's memory close. It had gone with Isaac on his first fishing voyage to the Grand Banks. It had gone with him to enlist in Washington's army. And it would cross the river with him tonight.

Back and forth, Isaac rowed. Every time he crossed to Long Island, he held his breath. Would the Redcoats be hiding in the fog to greet them with a hail of gunfire?

Ranger waited on shore for Isaac to take him wherever they were going. But one after another, the boats left without him.

Finally, Isaac's boat returned. "One more trip should do it," Joe whispered as Isaac climbed out of the boat to help the last group of men on board. Isaac was holding it steady but leaning against it, too, as if he needed it to keep himself up.

"You all right?" Joe asked him.

"Yes," Isaac said. "Just tired."

Ranger sloshed over and licked Isaac's hand. Sometimes he did that with Luke. When Luke was very tired or sick, it made him feel better to know that Ranger was there.

"You can come this time, dog," Isaac whispered. After the last man boarded, Isaac thumped his hand on the side of the boat, and Ranger jumped in.

"What's this?" an officer said, lifting the first aid kit from Ranger's neck. He opened it, took one look at the bandages inside, and let out a quiet huff of a laugh. "You suppose this will save us if the Redcoats catch up?" he whispered. "Five bandages and a —"

A hail of loud popping sounds interrupted him.

The officer stared toward shore, his eyes wide. Then he turned back to Isaac. "We must go!"

Isaac's entire body hurt. But what he saw when he looked up made him hurl himself into the boat. The Redcoats were pouring down the hill toward the river. Isaac scrambled to his feet and started rowing.

Isaac felt as if someone had a fist clenched around his heart. There was no way their little boats could outrun a British cannonball. He rowed as hard as he could. Every breath burned in his chest.

Keep rowing. Keep rowing, he thought. Isaac felt the dog at his side. Somehow, it helped calm his racing heart, even as the gunfire grew louder.

Ranger wanted to hide under a bench, but he stayed close to Isaac, even though the noise hurt his ears. It sounded like fireworks, but louder and with a sharp, dangerous smell.

"All right now!" the officer called when they were out of range of the British guns. The men rowing could finally slow their frantic pace.

When the boat brushed against the river bottom at the opposite shore, Isaac dropped his oar and collapsed.

Ranger ran to Isaac's side and licked his cheek. His skin was salty and hot. Too hot. Ranger nuzzled him to stand up. The other men were already marching up the bank.

Isaac tried to stand, but his knees buckled under him. His back felt as if it might split in two. His head pulsed with a sharp, throbbing pain that made everything blurry. He felt the dog's rough tongue on his cheek.

Then everything went black.

Chapter 4

FEVER DREAMS

When Isaac woke, he was in a barn. A few chickens clucked around, pecking at the floor.

Isaac leaned up on his elbows. Someone had spread a wool blanket in the hay to make a rough bed for him. Isaac looked around. His head throbbed. Where was Joe? Where was the rest of his regiment?

Isaac reached into his pocket and felt the scratchy rope against his palm. He remembered rowing through a hail of musket balls in the smoky morning fog. And then... nothing.

Wait. Had there been a dog? Or had that been a fever dream?

Isaac let out a soft whistle. "Dog?"

Ranger looked up. He had gone to get a drink of water from the trough, but he was glad to hear Isaac's voice. Isaac had been asleep for a long time. After he collapsed in the boat, Joe and the other soldiers had carried him to a tent full of other sick men. They'd given him medicine but Isaac just got sicker. For two days, Isaac had drifted in and out of restless sleep, until he woke one morning with dark red spots on his face and hands. One of the men helping shouted and ran from the tent. When he returned later that morning, soldiers came with him. They loaded Isaac into a cart and brought him here with the chickens.

Ranger had followed them the whole way. He didn't know where his first aid kit was anymore, but he knew that Isaac needed him.

"Dog? Are you here?" Isaac called again.

Ranger came over and nuzzled Isaac's shoulder.

"You *are* real," Isaac said, "and you're here!" But where was here, exactly?

Before Isaac could wonder for long, an older man shuffled into the barn with a tin cup of water and some bread.

Ranger trotted up to him and licked his hand.

"Good morning, pup," the farmer said. He set the water and bread down and knelt beside Ranger, scratching his neck with both wrinkled hands. Ranger leaned into the scratch. The man smelled like wood smoke and farm dust and bacon. He was a very good scratcher. Ranger was disappointed when he stopped and stood up to bring Isaac the water and bread.

"Here you go," the farmer said, handing Isaac the cup.

Isaac's hands trembled as he took a drink. How could he be so weak that a cup of water felt heavy? He set it down and looked at the farmer. "Thank you. But . . . I have to get back to my regiment."

"We have to get you better first, son," the farmer said. "Get some food in you." He nodded toward the bread.

Isaac reached for it and took a bite. As soon as the warm bread touched his lips, he realized how hungry he was. When was the last time he'd eaten? What was he doing here? "I appreciate your care, sir. But why was I brought here instead of the camp hospital?"

"You're under quarantine," the farmer said, "lest you spread this disease all through the Continental Army. I can care for you here because I've already had smallpox."

"Smallpox?" Isaac's voice trembled. He looked down at the spots on his hands, and his heart raced with panic. The disease had raged through Marblehead like a wildfire just three years before, killing neighbor after neighbor and terrifying the town. How could he have contracted smallpox? He couldn't be trapped here, sick. What if the troops had to cross another river?

Isaac struggled to his feet. He had to get out of this barn. He had to get back to his regiment. He had to get back to Joe and Colonel Glover and General Washington.

He staggered toward the door and collapsed. Ranger rushed to his side and sniffed at his face. Isaac was hot again.

The farmer eased Isaac back onto the blanket and held the cup to his lips until he took a tiny drink. "You'll get back to the army, son," he said quietly. "But first, you have to survive."

Chapter 5

A LONG, COLD ROAD

In the days that followed, Ranger stayed by Isaac's side. The bubbly rash that had started on the boy's hands spread until his whole body was covered with oozing bumps. His face and hands were the worst.

Every day, the farmer brought Isaac food and water. Ranger would lean close to him then, nudging Isaac to keep him alert while the farmer held the cup and urged him to take small sips.

It was two more weeks before Isaac's fever finally broke. But then the sores that covered his body hardened into thick, crusted scabs. Isaac couldn't move without crying out in pain.

Slowly, with Ranger at his side, Isaac began to eat and drink again. He was too weak to leave, but he began helping with barn chores. Ranger followed him around as he fed the chickens. Little by little, Isaac regained his strength until, finally, he was ready to return to the army.

It was mid-December when Isaac and Ranger set out to rejoin Isaac's unit. A messenger had brought word to the farm that the Fourteenth Continental Regiment was marching through New Jersey. He'd brought other news as well, and none of it was good.

The weeks that had been so terrible for Isaac had been just as painful for the Continental Army. The British had taken New York City. Washington's troops had been forced to retreat to New Jersey, and then Pennsylvania. Now they were just over the river from Trenton. But that city was held by the Hessians, paid German soldiers who fought with the Redcoats. General Washington feared the Hessians would cross the river and attack as soon as the ice formed. He'd ordered the Fourteenth to join the rest of the troops in Pennsylvania. And now, under the command of General John Sullivan, Isaac's regiment and others were marching to meet up with the rest of the army.

Isaac pulled his wool coat tight around him as they walked. The farmer had given him food and a bit of money for his journey. Isaac paid a man a few coins to ferry him and Ranger across the Hudson River.

They pressed on for another hour before it began to get dark. Isaac found a protected spot in the woods. He built a fire and shared a biscuit and dried meat with Ranger before they went to sleep.

In the morning, they set out again. Isaac thought he'd catch up with the rest of the troops in a day or two. But he and Ranger trudged through cold mud and slept two more nights in the woods, with no sign of General Sullivan's men.

The sun was low in the sky on December 20 when Isaac stopped. "Did you hear that, dog?" He stood still so his boots wouldn't rustle the dead leaves. It was quiet. Isaac shook his head. "Never mind," he said, and started walking again. "Come on, dog."

But Ranger didn't come. He tipped his head, listening. There was a noise, way in the distance. It sounded like the blowy music thing Sadie had brought home from school in third grade — all airy and high. Ranger barked.

Isaac turned around. "What is it?" He stopped, but all he heard was wind whistling through the bare trees. It was getting colder every minute, and soon it would be dark. Isaac shivered. They should have arrived at Washington's camp by now. Were they even going the right way anymore?

Ranger barked again. Then he started walking toward the sound.

"No, dog," Isaac said. "This way."

Ranger kept going until Isaac turned to follow him. The sound was getting louder. He smelled horses. And people. Lots of people. So many that he could feel the road vibrating under his paws.

"Wait!" Isaac paused to listen. It was fife music! And drumming. He looked down at Ranger. "Did you find General Sullivan?"

Find? Ranger's ears perked up. Sometimes it was hard to follow a person's scent, but today, it was easy. There were so many men! Their

scents were strong in the air and on the road — all sweat and blood and wood fires. Ranger kept his nose down and walked faster.

"Look!" Isaac shouted. Just down the hill, a long column of men marched ahead of them on the road.

Isaac's feet were so cold he could barely feel them anymore, but his heart warmed when he saw that the men were wearing the uniforms of the Continental Army.

When he caught up, an officer rode to meet him. "What is your business here?"

"I'm Isaac Pope of the Fourteenth Continental Regiment," Isaac said. "I fell ill as we ferried the army across the East River. A farmer cared for me until I was well again, and now I've come to rejoin my regiment."

"Very well." The officer looked Isaac up and down. "Fall in, then. There may be a special order for you when we arrive at camp."

"A special order?" Isaac was puzzled. "No one even knew I was on my way."

"Yes, but we've had a messenger meet us with a letter from General Washington," the officer said.

"General Washington?" What business could the general possibly have with him? "Are you certain he asked for me, sir?"

"He did not ask for you by name, but you may be suited to this job." The officer leaned down from his horse and lowered his voice. "The general is in need of a spy."

Chapter 6

SOLDIERS AND SPIES

In another hour, they arrived at Washington's camp — a sea of canvas tents with soldiers milling about in the twilight. Isaac breathed in the smell of soup, simmering in big kettles over the fires, and realized how hungry he'd been. The farmer's biscuits hadn't lasted long.

Isaac was about to go looking for Joe when the officer he met on the road appeared at his side. "Follow me." The man led Isaac to a tent that was larger than the rest. He lifted the flap, and Isaac stepped inside. Ranger started to follow, but the officer blocked him with a big leather boot. "The hound can wait outside," he said.

The officer folded his arms and looked at Isaac. "Although you were separated from your unit, you must know that our situation is desperate," he said.

Isaac nodded. He'd heard enough to know that the Continental Army was in trouble. Many expected that the Redcoats would take Philadelphia any day.

"We must have a victory to keep the cause alive," the officer said.

Isaac felt a strange weight settle over him. Did the officer expect *him* to deliver that victory? "How may I be of help, sir?"

The officer pulled a letter from his cloak. "Recently, General Washington wrote to his officers asking us to find a man who might cross the river as a spy without being detected," he said. He unfolded the letter and read, "That we may, if possible, obtain some knowledge of the enemy's situation, movements, and intention. Particular inquiry should be made by the person sent, if any preparations are being made to cross the river."

"But, sir . . ." Isaac's empty stomach twisted. He had never imagined himself a spy. As soon as he did, it was easy to imagine himself being captured. "Surely there is a local man who would better know the area and —"

"The general fears that someone local might betray us." The officer looked at Isaac. "Beyond that, you are in a special position to enter the Hessians' camp."

Isaac stared at the officer. "How is that, sir?"

The officer looked Isaac up and down. "We will dress you in the clothes of a butcher's servant. As such, you shall deliver meat to the Hessian regiments at Trenton," he said. "If they are as hungry as we are, you will be most

welcome. You must find the Hessian commander, Colonel Rall. Tell him that you are a slave who has escaped from your master. And that the British hired you to spy on the Rebels, so you have come with information as well as pork."

Now Isaac understood why he'd been chosen. The Redcoats had offered freedom to any enslaved man who ran from a Rebel and joined them. Isaac had seen plenty of men with brown skin fighting with the British on Long Island. And who could blame them? The Continental Army offered no such promises. Men like Joe were fighting for freedom they might never have for themselves.

But Isaac had pledged his loyalty to the Patriot cause. The mariners of Marblehead were like brothers. He'd promised to stand beside them to the end. If this was what he was called upon to do, then he would obey the order.

"I understand, sir," Isaac said. "When shall I go?"

"You will cross the river tonight," the officer said. "Pay attention to the activities of the Hessians and the terrain on the way to Trenton as well. It may all be of use."

Ranger sat close to the tent, listening to the muffled voices inside. When Isaac finally came back, his eyes were wide and scared. Ranger nuzzled his hand until Isaac looked down and scratched his neck.

"Wish me luck, dog," he said. "I hope I see you again."

"Take him with you," someone said. Isaac looked up and saw the officer leaning out of the tent. "Tell the Hessians you stole him from your master. If the dog comes back here alone, we'll know you've run into trouble." The officer handed Isaac his disguise — a shirt and trousers, a wool blanket, and a blood-stained leather apron like the one the butcher had worn back home in Marblehead. "Get dressed and be off."

Isaac went to a tent and changed his clothes, shivering in the cold wind that blew through the canvas. He wrapped the blanket around his shoulders and looked down at Ranger. "Ready, dog?"

Ranger followed Isaac out of camp. As they walked, voices and cooking noises faded into the trees until the only sound was the crunch of Isaac's shoes in the crusty snow.

Isaac pulled the knotted rope from his pocket and held it as he marched. Ranger sniffed at it. It smelled a little like the thick rope Luke and Sadie used to play tug-of-war with him sometimes. Did Isaac want to play?

Ranger grabbed the rope in his teeth and yanked it out of Isaac's hand.

"Hey!" Isaac reached for it but missed.

Ranger shook the rope in his mouth. Isaac laughed and dove for it. He caught one end and tugged, but Ranger held on. "You want to play, do you?" They yanked the rope back and forth until, finally, Isaac stopped to catch his breath.

"That was fun, but we have to keep going now," he said. He gave a gentle tug, and Ranger followed him along the trail. Neither one of them let go of the knotted rope until they reached the Delaware River. Then, Isaac dropped it and stared.

General Washington's fears had come true. The river had iced over in the frigid weather. Isaac was surprised the Hessians hadn't already crossed to attack them. But they hadn't.

Now it was up to Isaac to make sure they never did.

Chapter 7

RIVER RESCUE!

Isaac picked up the rope and shoved it into his pocket. Then he stepped carefully onto the ice. It held. He took another step. And another. The farther he got from shore, the more his heart thudded in his chest, as if it didn't want to come along on this dangerous trip. But Isaac had been given an order.

Ranger followed Isaac out onto the ice. He'd walked on ice plenty of times before, when Luke and Sadie went out to play hockey on the frozen pond near their house. But this ice felt different. Slushy and uneven. Dangerous.

Ranger barked, and Isaac hesitated. Ranger pawed at Isaac's leg and barked again. It wasn't safe. They should go back.

"It's okay, dog." Isaac squinted into the darkness. "We're more than halfway." He could make out a light on the other shore. Maybe a lantern in a tavern or ferry building. Were the Hessians inside? He'd have to be ready with his story if they came out to confront him.

Isaac started walking again, sliding his feet over the river's icy surface so he wouldn't slip and fall. When he met the Hessian soldiers, he'd make sure his apron was showing. I've come with information, he'd say, as if they should already know who he was. When they didn't, he'd explain that he worked for the British, and —

Crack!

The ice under Isaac's feet buckled. He froze.

Water seeped up from the river as the crack spread like a spider web beneath him.

Isaac sucked in his breath. Could he go back? Slowly, he turned to look at Ranger. The dog crouched, whimpering on the ice nearby.

"It's all right, dog," Isaac said. But his voice trembled and his heart raced.

It wasn't all right. None of this was all right.

But if he moved slowly enough, maybe he could get back to solid ice.

Isaac slid one foot to the side. The ice seemed stable, but as soon as he shifted his weight, there was another crack, and the ice chunk tilted. His boots slipped out from under him.

No!

A wave of river water rushed over the ice as Isaac fell. He threw his arms out and tried to grab something — anything — to claw his way to safety. But there was nothing to hold.

Isaac plunged into the icy river. It was so cold he couldn't breathe. He couldn't even think. But he caught another slab of ice floating by and held on.

Ranger barked. His paws slid as he tried to stay afloat on his own chunk of ice that had suddenly broken free. Just as he caught his balance, another slab came churning down the river and slammed into his, throwing him into the water.

Ranger paddled as hard as he could. He strained to lift his head so he could see. Where was Isaac?

There! Isaac was clinging to a piece of ice floating downstream. More ice was breaking free every second — enormous chunks bigger than horses. The rushing river sent them

crashing into one another. Isaac had to get to shore or he'd be crushed!

Ranger paddled toward Isaac. The current had brought them closer to the New Jersey shore. It wasn't too far to swim. Ranger barked and pawed at Isaac's shoulder. But Isaac wouldn't let go.

Ranger barked again. He swam toward shore a little and then back. Isaac needed to follow him!

"Go on, dog!" Isaac's voice shook. He lifted a shaky hand and pointed toward shore. "Go on!" Maybe the dog would bring help. Isaac tried not to think about what would happen if the Hessians who rescued him found out he was a spy. He'd be killed for treason. But at least he'd get out of the river. He didn't know how much longer he could hold on.

"Go on, dog! Go!" Isaac shouted. But the

dog kept coming back to him. "I can't swim! Go! Find help!"

Find? Ranger didn't want to leave Isaac, but he couldn't make him let go of the ice. He'd have to find someone to help.

Ranger turned and paddled for shore. The river churned with ice chunks bumping together. Ranger swam between them until he felt rocks under his paws and scrambled onto the icy bank.

Ranger shook himself. He looked around.

The shore was quiet. But along with the smells of river ice and wood smoke in the air, Ranger picked up the scent of men. Two of the scent trails were fresh. Someone had been here not long ago. Ranger had to find them — quickly! He had to bring them to help Isaac.

Ranger followed the scent trail along the shore and through some trees. He followed it up a long, rocky hill to a road.

There! Two men in dark coats and pointy hats were walking away from him. Ranger barked, and one of them turned around.

Ranger ran up to the men. One bent to pet him. The other said something. His words sounded different from the way Luke and Sadie and Isaac talked.

Ranger pawed at the men's legs. He ran back and forth barking until, finally, one of the men said something and they both started toward the river.

Ranger led them down the bank to the shore. All he saw was water and ice.

The men talked to each other and started to go away. Ranger jumped up on one of them and barked again. He raced up and down the riverbank. Where was Isaac?

Finally, a weak voice called out, "Dog? Here!"

Ranger raced down the shoreline with the

soldiers rushing after him. Isaac had made it through the ice and collapsed on the river-bank. He was shivering in his frozen clothes and could barely speak. But he reached out to Ranger.

Ranger licked the boy's hand and then huddled close to warm him.

The two soldiers shouted something at Isaac.

"What?" Isaac's eyes were wide. He held his shaking hands up and pointed toward Trenton. "I have information. I need to see Colonel Rall," he said. He could barely get the words out through his chattering teeth.

The men looked at each other. One took a wool blanket from his sack and wrapped it around Isaac. Then he pulled Isaac roughly to his feet. He spoke to the other man, and they led Isaac up the hill.

Isaac didn't understand German. All he could do was hope they were taking him to the Hessian headquarters and Colonel Rall. When he got there, he'd have one chance to convince the Hessian commander he was a friend. One chance to stay alive.

Chapter 8

LIFE-OR-DEATH LIES

Isaac's feet were numb, but he forced himself to keep walking with the Hessian soldiers. He'd been half-asleep on the riverbank, so cold that he thought of closing his eyes and giving up. But then the dog had found him. The Hessians had warmed him at a fire until he was painfully awake. Every bit of his skin burned with the cold now as they set out for Trenton.

Isaac wished he could sink down in the snow and go to sleep. But he had to stay alert. He was already gathering information about the road.

He noticed how the steep, icy trail wound its way through dark woods. The ruts would make travel difficult for horses, carts, and cannons. Isaac noted the two ravines they crossed — one deep and one smaller. He tried to etch every detail into his memory.

When they arrived in Trenton, Ranger followed Isaac and the soldiers into a house. It smelled of wood smoke and meat and pine branches. A stern-looking man sat in a chair by the fire. He wore a ruffled shirt under his jacket and a scowl on his face. It had to be Colonel Rall.

Isaac started to speak, but one of the soldiers held up a hand and said something. The other man left the room, and a few minutes later, he returned with a different soldier who spoke both German and English. This man would serve as a translator.

The soldier nodded for Isaac to begin, so he

launched into the story he'd rehearsed. He said he'd been chased by a Patriot patrol and tried to escape across the river, but then the ice broke. Isaac paused so the soldier could translate.

Colonel Rall laughed and said something to the others. Isaac looked at the man translating. "We check the ice every day," he said. "We test if it is safe to cross. Not yet."

Isaac nodded. He tried not to look interested, but this was important information. It was just as General Washington feared! The Hessians were only waiting for solid ice to form. Then they would cross the river and attack. Isaac swallowed hard and went on with his story.

When he fell through the ice, he told the soldiers, he heard the men who had chased him laughing and jeering on the opposite shore. They must have been certain he'd die in the icy water. And he would have, except for the dog that went to get the Hessian soldiers to save him.

Colonel Rall looked at Ranger. He looked at the soldiers who had found Isaac, and they nodded. This was indeed what had happened.

Colonel Rall said something and pointed to the door. One of the soldiers let Ranger outside, with some other dogs that were in the yard.

Then the translator looked at Isaac and said, "Where did you come from?"

Isaac's heart thudded, but he forced his voice to stay calm as he told the rest of his story. How he'd escaped from the butcher who enslaved him and been hired as a British spy. How he'd spent time in Washington's camp and was here now to report on the activities there.

The translator explained all this to Rall, who said something in reply. The translator looked at Isaac. "So now you are here. What do you have to report?"

Isaac delivered the lie he'd practiced. "I have seen Washington's men in their winter quarters," he said. "They are in a sad state, hungry and weak. Their spirits are as broken as their bodies. Many are refusing orders. The officers can no longer control them."

Rall leaned back in his chair and smiled. He said something to the other men, who laughed. Isaac looked at the translator, who said, "The colonel is not surprised. But he is pleased that he did not waste time building fortifications around Trenton as General Cornwallis ordered. He has known all along that Washington's country clowns would never dare to attack."

Anger burned in Isaac's chest. He reached into his pocket and squeezed the frozen, knotted rope. He had to stay calm. He couldn't give himself away. He clenched his jaw and nodded. "They would be hard-pressed to defend themselves, much less launch an attack."

Suddenly, Colonel Rall leaned forward, studying Isaac's face. His eyes narrowed when he spoke.

"He asks how he can be sure that you tell the truth," the translator said. "How are we to know that you are not a spy for the Continental Army?"

Isaac's stomach leaped into his throat. Had his anger shown in his eyes? He wanted to run. But they were waiting for his answer.

"Does the colonel suppose that a spy would cross the river in broad daylight?" Isaac forced out a laugh. "That would be a foolish spy indeed." He felt Colonel Rall's eyes on him and looked away, out the window.

Ranger was there, playing with the Hessians' dogs. A young soldier was tossing snowballs,

and the dogs were leaping to bite them. Isaac pointed. "Surely your hounds would have sniffed out a Patriot dog in their ranks."

Colonel Rall looked out the window just as Ranger leaped into the air to catch a snowball. It exploded into a shower of snow that stuck to the fur on his chin. Ranger sat down and pawed at his frozen, white beard. The colonel smiled. Then he turned to his men and spoke.

The translator waited, then asked, "Can you get close enough to observe Washington's men again?"

"Of course," Isaac answered.

The man nodded. "You shall stay with us tonight. In the morning, when your clothes are dry, you will go. You will return to us in three days' time to share all that we need to know to launch our attack."

Chapter 9

A SECRET PLAN

Isaac spent a fitful night on the floor of one of the Trenton homes the Hessians had taken over. Would they really let him walk away in the morning? Or did they suspect that he wasn't really a friend? Running off in the night would give him away as a spy, for sure. So Isaac stayed, stroking Ranger's fur to calm himself.

"Come on, dog!" Isaac called when it was time to leave in the morning. His clothes had dried by the fire overnight. He changed into them, and he and Ranger began the long walk back to the river. The closer they got, the faster

Isaac's heart beat as he thought about crossing again.

It had been a cold night. The ice *should* be thicker now. But the memory of plunging into that frigid water was fresh in his bones.

And what if the ice was gone completely? There was no hope of finding a boat. After General Washington had brought his men across from Trenton, he'd seized or burned every boat within seventy miles so the Hessians couldn't follow them.

When they reached the river, Isaac let out a long breath. It was frozen clear to the Pennsylvania shore. But his sense of relief didn't last. That meant he'd have to cross the thin ice again to return to Washington's camp.

Ranger sniffed at the rocks on shore. He barked and pawed at Isaac's leg.

"I know, dog." Isaac reached down to pat Ranger's head. "But we have a job to do." He reminded himself of the information he was bringing back to camp. He had to make it. If he didn't, everything he'd learned would be lost.

Isaac took a careful step onto the river. It felt solid. But it had felt that way before.

Ranger slid a paw onto the ice and whimpered. He didn't want to go on the frozen river again. But Isaac was crossing. And that meant Ranger had to cross, too.

Step by careful step, Isaac made his way across. Once, the ice beneath his feet let out a loud crack and a hiss. Isaac froze in his tracks. But the ice held, and soon he and Ranger were climbing the snowy bank on the far shore.

When they arrived back at camp, Isaac had never felt so grateful to see the tents of the Continental Army. An officer hurried out to greet them.

"Have you news from Trenton?" he asked.

Isaac nodded, and the officer motioned for him to come inside a tent. "The general wishes to see you."

General Washington? Isaac's eyes widened. He looked down at Ranger. "Stay, dog. Stay."

"No need for that. Bring him inside," a deep voice called from the tent.

Isaac's breath caught in his throat. General Washington himself stood at the entrance. His height and wool cloak were unmistakable. He held the tent open and slapped his thigh.

Ranger trotted up and sniffed General Washington's hand. He smelled like wood smoke and wet wool. Other dogs, too.

Isaac followed Ranger into the tent. Half a dozen officers sat around a long wooden table covered in papers and maps. "Very well, then," said one of the officers, looking at Isaac. "What have you to report?"

Isaac stood up straighter. "The Hessians have been watching the ice on the river," he said. He told them how he'd fallen through and ended up by Colonel Rall's fire. He told them about the walk to Trenton — the long, windy stretches, the rutted road, and the ravines.

"How many men are there?" an officer asked.

"I'm not certain." Isaac thought about what he'd seen. "More than a thousand, but less than two, I think."

Washington nodded. "Is there anything more?"

"I told Colonel Rall that your army has no plans to move. That the men are hungry and weak and no longer following orders." Isaac hesitated. He wasn't sure if he should share the colonel's response. "Colonel Rall called our men 'country clowns.' He said he'd been ordered to build fortifications but didn't, because he knew you wouldn't attack. They told me to observe your camp and return to them in three days with information. In three days. I believe that's when they plan to cross the river to attack us." Isaac felt the weight of what he'd just said. He'd gone into enemy territory as a spy and learned that the fiercest of all the troops fighting for King George were on their way to attack.

"Very well," General Washington said quietly. He looked at Isaac. "Thank you for your courage, lad. This information is most helpful." He looked to his officers. "We will meet for a council of war tonight." Then he turned back to Isaac. "Not a word of this to anyone."

Isaac knew he should leave, but he couldn't help asking, "Was my information truly useful? Will it help us prepare for the Hessians' attack?"

"The Hessians will not be attacking," General Washington said.

"They won't?" Isaac was confused. Didn't the officers believe him?

"They will not," the general said. "Because we are going to attack first."

Chapter 10

CHRISTMAS CROSSING

On Christmas morning, Isaac woke to the smell of cook fires. When he ventured out from the tent, his boots made dark prints in the fresh snow.

"Well, look who's back with us!" Joe's deep voice boomed. He rushed to Isaac's side and clapped a hand on his shoulder. "A merry Christmas to you, my friend. Are you well?"

Isaac hesitated. He wanted to tell Joe where he'd been, what he'd done, and what was about to happen. But General Washington's voice echoed in his mind.

Not a word of this to anyone.

"I am well," Isaac said. "And a merry Christmas to you, too."

It hardly felt like Christmas. At home in Marblehead, there would have been meat pies baking and bells ringing in the churches. Here in camp, the chaplains called men together for simple, quiet services.

Later in the day, the officers passed out fresh flints for the muskets, along with powder, musket balls, blankets, and three days' worth of food. No one had announced General Washington's plan, but as soon as Isaac was handed his rations, he knew. They would be crossing the river tonight.

Early in the afternoon, the soldiers gathered at the parade grounds, ready to march. Every man carried a musket — even the fifers and drummers. They were told to bring sixty rounds of cartridges and as much ammunition as they could carry. Isaac filled his cartridge box and stuffed the rest into his coat pockets. He got in line and began the long, snowy trudge to the river.

Ranger walked alongside Isaac and Joe. The air felt different today. Something was happening. Ranger didn't know what, but he knew he needed to stay by Isaac's side.

Ranger sniffed the air as they walked. It smelled of ice and river water and tired men. Some marched even though they'd been sick, even though they could barely walk. Some had worn out their shoes and left bloody footprints in the snow.

The wind picked up all through the afternoon. Isaac pulled his blanket tighter around his shoulders and shivered. He couldn't stop thinking about how cold and biting the river had been when he fell through the ice.

At four o'clock, with a clouded sun low in

the sky, all the troops gathered at the river. Finally, the officers shared the truth. The Continental Army would cross the Delaware River tonight while the Hessians slept.

Isaac stood tall while Colonel Glover explained their impossible task. The soldiers of the Fourteenth Continental Regiment would man the boats. They would have to deliver more than two thousand men, plus horses and artillery, across the river before sunrise. Only then could the march to Trenton begin.

For three weeks, Washington had been hiding the flat-bottomed boats he'd seized in inlets and creeks, and on islands that were thick with trees. Now the boats were lined up on shore. They were about forty feet long and eight feet wide. Each one would fit around forty men, standing close together.

Isaac stood in the cold rain, waiting for orders. Their mission had just begun, but already they'd fallen behind schedule. They had hoped to launch the first boats at dusk, but ice floes in the river had delayed them. The ice had broken up since Isaac's last crossing. Now it came barreling down the river in giant chunks that piled up on one another. They'd have to wait for an opening to cross.

Isaac watched the ice careening down the river. His heart thudded in his chest. He'd tried to tell himself this would be no different from crossing the East River that night back on Long Island. But that had been August. Tonight, they'd have to cross in the middle of a fierce winter storm.

Ranger's fur was dripping wet. His paws stung from the ice that had worked its way between his toes. But he stayed at Isaac's side until, finally, the order came. It was time to load the first boats and push off from shore.

Isaac was assigned to a team with Joe and

four other Marblehead men. He held their boat steady as soldier after soldier climbed aboard. Ranger tried to jump in, too, but Isaac blocked his way. "There's no room now, dog. You'll cross with me later on." When the boat was full, Isaac pushed off with one of the long oars. In shallow water, the men used them as poles, pushing against the river bottom to move the boat.

Ranger whined as he watched Isaac pull away from shore. In an instant, the boat vanished into the swirling rain and snow. Ranger stood on the bank and waited. He watched other men load other boats, and those disappeared, too. When would Isaac come back?

When the water was deep enough, Isaac and the other men switched from poling to rowing. Once the Pennsylvania shore disappeared into the storm, Isaac couldn't see land at all — just swirling snow and great hunks of ice that came surging down the river. The men did their best to hold them off with the oars, but huge slabs slammed into the side of the boat. Isaac felt every jolt. What if the boats were dashed to pieces before they made it to the other side?

Finally, Isaac saw a glimmer of light in the distance. His heart flooded with relief, but only for a moment. What if it was a Hessian patrol? What if Hessian guards were waiting on the opposite shore? It would be impossible for them to land without being seen. Isaac's heart pumped faster with every pull of the oars.

But there was no turning back. He had an order to follow. He had to get these men across the river, no matter what was waiting on the other side.

Chapter 11

A RACE AGAINST TIME

As the light grew near, Isaac saw that it was coming from the Johnson Ferry House, and he breathed a sigh of relief. He knew from men in camp that the ferry house was owned by friends. And there were no Hessian soldiers waiting when the boat scraped the river bottom. Only an empty bank, swirling with rain and snow.

Isaac and Joe held the boat while the soldiers climbed out. Then the men of the Fourteenth Continental Regiment pushed away from shore and started back across the river. Ranger was waiting for Isaac on the other side. He splashed into the river, jumped up on the edge of the boat, and licked Isaac's hand. But once again, Isaac shook his head. "Stay, dog. Stay." Once the boat was loaded, they pushed off again.

Back and forth Isaac rowed. Every so often, he caught Joe's eye, and his friend would give him a quiet nod.

With every hour, the storm grew more intense. It rained and snowed and sleeted. Wind howled through the tunnel of trees that lined the riverbank. Isaac was glad to be rowing. At least the work kept him warm. The men who huddled together in the boat were frozen half to death.

"Keep moving, gentlemen!" a voice boomed as another group of men boarded the boats. It was General Knox, the officer Washington had put in charge of the crossing. He paced back and forth on shore. Isaac wished he could make the boats cross more quickly, but there was no arguing with ice. Huge, flat chunks came spinning down the river, pushing the boats farther downstream. They were way behind schedule.

All Isaac could do was keep rowing. His hands were cracked and bleeding. But Colonel Glover had made a promise. "My mariners will deliver your men across that river," he'd told Washington. He had faith in the men of the Fourteenth Continental Regiment. Isaac did, too.

All night long, they navigated back and forth. They had relied on one another in the middle of storms in the Grand Banks. They understood that if one man failed to follow an order, the whole boat could go down. They worked together, young and old, black and white.

It wasn't like that in the rest of the army. In the early days, General Washington himself had argued that black men shouldn't be recruited as soldiers. Now the Patriots were desperate and welcomed everyone, free or enslaved. But there was no promise that enslaved men like Joe who enlisted with the Continental Army would be free when the war ended. That's why many had run to join the British. It had seemed so foolish of General Washington not to welcome every soldier he could get.

Isaac wondered if their enlistments would be so low now if the general had been more thoughtful. He pulled on the ice-coated oar and wondered how outnumbered they would be when they marched on Trenton.

When the last group of men boarded the boat, there was still room, so Isaac thumped the railing with his hand. "Come on, dog!"

Ranger sloshed into the river. He tried to jump into the boat, but the sides were too high. Isaac had to grab him around his belly and lift him in. Soon, Isaac was pushing away from shore, and they began the crossing.

Ranger hated boats. They bobbed and tipped too much. They made his paws feel all wobbly beneath him. Ranger didn't even like going on the boat at home with Luke and Sadie and their friends. And this boat was nothing like that.

Huge chunks of ice came barreling toward them. One hit the side of the boat with a thud. Soldiers clutched the railing with red, raw hands.

Isaac strained his eyes to see when the next huge slab might appear. The ice floes were mostly invisible, but he caught a shimmer of white above the water.

This was going to be a big one.

Chapter 12

MAN OVERBOARD!

"Push off!" Isaac shouted. The other men tried to maneuver the boat away from the ice careening toward them, but there was no time. An officer standing next to Ranger pulled his sword from his belt and thrust it out, as if the ice were an enemy who might surrender. The ice kept coming. The officer tried to push it away with his blade, but the tip got stuck. He wrenched it free, and when he pulled his sword back into the boat, the tip was gone.

Before the officer could put his sword away, another slab of ice thumped into them. The boat bucked like a restless horse. A soldier lost his balance and stumbled into Ranger. Then someone shouted, "Man overboard! Grab his hand!"

Ranger jumped up with his paws on the rail so he could see. It was Joe! Somehow in the chaos, he'd fallen over the rail. Now he was thrashing at the river's surface. Icy water swirled around him. He could barely keep his head up. Another man stretched out his arm, but it didn't reach. The current was pushing Joe away from the boat.

"Joe!" Isaac tossed him the end of a rope, but Joe was flailing his arms so wildly, he knocked it away. He was already starting to go under.

Ranger leaped over the rail into the water.

Even with Ranger's thick fur, the icy water took away his breath.

Where was the rope? Ranger spotted it

nearby, but it was moving fast in the current. Ranger paddled as hard as he could until he reached it. He grabbed it in his teeth and swam toward Joe. But Joe wouldn't reach out to take it. Ranger pushed it at him, but he just slapped frantically at the waves. Ranger was afraid Joe would grab him and pull him underwater. But he had to make him take the rope!

Ranger barked and the rope dropped from his mouth. He snatched it up again and pushed it into Joe's face. Joe sputtered, but he stopped flopping long enough to grab it. Ranger started swimming back to the boat.

"He's got it!" an officer shouted. "Haul him in!"

Isaac pulled the rope, hand over hand, until Joe was close enough to reach. Then two other soldiers grabbed him and hoisted him over the railing. Another man wrapped him in a blanket.

Ranger was still in the icy river. He paddled closer to the boat. He barked, but no one noticed. The water was pushing him away, and he couldn't get his paws up on the rail.

Ranger struggled to keep his head above the icy water. He barked again, and Isaac's face appeared over the railing.

"Dog!" He leaned way down, grabbed Ranger under his front legs, and hauled him onto the boat.

Ranger shook himself off while Isaac scrambled for his oar.

"Watch out! Big one!" someone cried. Isaac barely saw the next ice floe before it slammed into the bow, knocking them off course.

Isaac's palms burned with blisters, but he pulled harder on the oar. Every time he and the other men made progress, another chunk of ice clunked into the boat and pushed them downriver.

But finally, they straightened their course and made it to shore. Isaac held the boat while the men climbed out.

"Come on, dog," Isaac said when only Ranger was left in the boat. But Ranger didn't move. He wanted to see what Isaac would do. Was he staying here or going back?

Isaac thumped the railing with his hand. "Let's go! Out!"

Ranger just looked at him. Finally, Isaac leaned into the boat, grabbed Ranger around his middle, and lugged him over the railing.

"Stay," Isaac said. Then he and Joe climbed back into the boat. The soldiers were all here now, but there were horses and guns left to move.

"Make haste, gentlemen!" a deep voice called. General Washington stood at the river's edge, looking down at his pocket watch.

"We won't make Trenton before dawn. Not even close," an officer said. "What now?"

"Now," the general answered, "we wait for these fine men to return." He looked at Isaac and the other mariners. "When I march into Trenton, I shall do so with all of you at my side."

As the boat started back across the river, Ranger walked up the bank to a clearing where some men had built a fire. They stood quietly in the smoke, rubbing their red hands together. Their faces were serious and scared. One of the men sat down beside Ranger and put an arm around him. Ranger could feel the man's heart thumping through his wet coat.

Finally, the boats returned with horses, carts, and cannons. Where was Isaac? Ranger wandered through the troops until he found him, lining up with his musket over his shoulder. When Isaac saw Ranger, he reached down to scratch his neck. Then their marching order came from the front.

Joe clapped a hand on Isaac's shoulder. "You ready, my friend?"

Isaac nodded. He looked down at Ranger. "Ready, dog? It's time."

Chapter 13

NO TURNING BACK

Isaac wrapped his wool blanket around his shoulders. He'd stood by the fire for a few minutes but barely had time to warm up. Already, his blanket was crusted with ice.

It was four in the morning — more than three hours later than they'd planned to set out from the river. There was no hope of arriving in darkness now. They'd march into Trenton in full daylight. If the Hessians got word of their approach, it would be a massacre.

The orders had been made clear from the first step. March at a brisk pace. Wrap blankets around the muskets to keep the firing mechanisms dry. And no man was allowed to leave. Anyone who tried would face instant punishment.

It was nine miles to Trenton. Isaac and the others marched up the bank from the river. The road was icy and rutted as it wound through the dark woods. Isaac wished the night could last longer to hide their approach. Once dawn arrived, how could the Hessians miss a mile-long column of men?

When they reached the crossroad at Bear Tavern, the troops turned. The road was still slick, but it was level, and they began to make better time. The storm wasn't blowing right in their faces anymore, but no matter how tightly he pulled the blanket around him, Isaac couldn't get warm. It was getting harder and harder to keep up. Joe had already stayed back to help a man who was injured.

Before long, the whole line of men came to a halt. Isaac found himself staring down into one of the ravines he'd seen when he made this journey before. A rocky creek bed stretched out a hundred feet below the road. Crossing it would cost them more time.

But thanks to the information Isaac had brought back from his spy mission, the officers had a plan. One by one, men unharnessed the horses and prepared the artillery. Isaac helped them attach drag ropes to the trees. The men used these to lower cannons to the bottom of the ravine and haul them up on the other side. Time seemed to stand still as the snow and ice swirled, but finally, they made it across.

The clock hadn't stopped, though. It would be light long before they made it to Trenton. They'd only marched a short way when they came to the second ravine, smaller and steeper than the first. It slowed them down even more.

Finally, they set out on the road again, wide open to the wind and snow. Ranger nudged Isaac whenever he slowed down. All around them, soldiers were shivering and dragging their feet. One man quietly slipped out of line, stumbled off the road, and collapsed. Ranger started toward him, but Isaac grabbed his collar. "Stay, dog."

Ranger barked. Hadn't Isaac seen the man fall? Hadn't anyone? The line of men just kept marching in a tired trance.

As soon as Isaac let go, Ranger broke away and ran to the man by the side of the road. Ranger nuzzled his hand, but he didn't move. Ranger barked. The man didn't respond. By then, all the troops had marched on by.

Ranger ran ahead to the soldiers and jumped up on one of them.

"Down!" The man swatted him away, but Ranger kept barking. He went back and forth from the man in the snow to the troops. That was what you did when someone was in trouble and you needed to bring help. Ranger had practiced in his training with Luke and Dad. He'd followed Luke's scent to wherever he was hiding in the woods, pretending to be lost and hurt. When he found Luke, he'd barked to give the alert.

But sometimes that wasn't enough. When you were a search-and-rescue dog, sometimes you had to leave the person you found and go get a helper. Then you brought them back to the person who was hurt or sick.

The man in the snow was in trouble, so Ranger kept running back and forth. Finally, an officer stopped. "That dog has found something," he said. He pointed down the road and ordered two of his men, "Follow him and make sure it's not a Hessian spy!"

Ranger led the men to the soldier who had

fallen. He was covered in snow, nearly hidden. Ranger pawed at the man's shoulder.

The soldiers hurried to the man's side and wrapped him in their blankets. When he began to stir, they helped him stand and loaded him onto one of their horses to ride back to the troops.

Ranger didn't wait for anyone to pat him on the head or tell him what a good dog he was. At home, when Ranger trained with Luke and Dad, he got ear scratches and hugs when he'd done a good job. But this icy road was a long way from home. Ranger didn't even know where his first aid kit was. But he knew his work wasn't done.

Ranger raced up to find Isaac. He fell into step beside him and licked his cold fingers. Isaac looked down, but all he could do was sigh and lay his hand on the dog's ice-crusted head. It felt as if this frigid death march would never end.

Finally, they stopped at another crossroads. Here, the officers explained, they would split into two groups and take two different roads into Trenton. The plan was to surround the town and attack while the Hessians were still sleeping.

Isaac wondered if their weapons would even work. The men had sent word up to the front of the column, warning General Washington that the guns might be too wet to fire by the time they arrived.

Word came back from Washington almost immediately. His order was clear. "Advance and charge." Whether the guns worked or not, they were going.

There would be no turning back.

Chapter 14

THE BATTLE OF TRENTON

The sky began to grow light as Isaac and the other men on the River Road marched toward Trenton. Half an hour after sunrise, there was gunfire in the distance. Then a cannon blast. Hessian kettledrums boomed in the center of town. It was a call to arms. The battle was beginning.

Gunfire erupted just up ahead. "Into the fields!" came an order from the front. Isaac scrambled off the road and took cover behind a tree stump. Ranger stayed low at his side.

The air smelled dangerous and sharp — like fire and cold metal and fear.

Isaac's hands trembled as he loaded his musket. Would it even work after this night of rain and wind?

"The Hessian guards are firing on us!" someone shouted. "They're advancing! Fix your bayonets!"

Isaac held his gun and attached the bayonet, the long, sharp blade that fit underneath its muzzle for hand-to-hand fighting. He shuddered, imagining himself close enough to a Hessian soldier to use it.

"Advance!" General Sullivan shouted.

Isaac scrambled to his feet and ran into the road.

There was gunfire and shouting. Smoke swirled in the wind with the ice and rain.

Isaac's heart raced with terror as he rushed forward with the other men. Ranger tried to stay with him but there were so many soldiers, so many pounding feet in the snow.

"They're retreating!" someone shouted.

There! Ranger spotted Isaac running up the side of the road as they chased the Hessians toward town. Ranger ran up to him and nudged his hand so Isaac would know he was there.

"Go on, dog!" Isaac didn't slow down, but he waved Ranger away with his hand. "Get out of here. You don't want to be in the middle of this."

Ranger was good at following commands. That was important in search-and-rescue training. But he wouldn't follow this one. If Isaac was going to keep running toward the loud noises and smoke, Ranger was going, too.

General Sullivan's troops chased the Hessians all the way into Trenton. Isaac needed to reload his musket, but there was nowhere safe to stand still. The center of town boomed with cannon fire. Sounds of splintering wood and shattering glass filled the streets. Isaac ducked behind a barrel near a brick building and reached for his cartridge bag.

Ranger stood beside him. His fur prickled all over. The fireworks noises hurt his ears. He wished he were home in the mudroom, where he could hide in his dog bed until it stopped. He didn't know how to protect Isaac in this awful, loud place where men ran every-where. But he couldn't leave him alone.

Isaac finished loading his musket and joined the stream of soldiers running past. The Hessians seemed to have abandoned the town. Everywhere Isaac looked, Continental soldiers had taken over houses and basements. Had they done it? Had they managed to storm Trenton before the Hessians could organize to defend it?

"Take cover!" someone shouted as gunfire erupted again.

A burning pain seared through Isaac's leg. He dove behind a fence and pressed his hand to his thigh. It was wet and warm with blood. Isaac clenched his teeth. He peered out from between the posts, and his breath caught in his chest. An entire Hessian regiment, under fire from the other direction, was rushing toward them.

Isaac's leg throbbed. He felt dizzy, but he lifted his musket to his shoulder and tried to hold it steady. Before he could even shoot, the Hessian lines began to break. Continental soldiers were firing from the houses and basements where they were hiding.

"To the bridge!" someone shouted. "They're trying to escape over the creek!"

Isaac limped behind the rest of the soldiers as they raced with their muskets to the stone

bridge. One group of Hessians had already made it across. Instead of chasing them, Glover ordered his men to take the high ground south of the creek.

"Ready the guns!" Glover shouted. Isaac's legs felt like they might crumble beneath him, but he heaved on the ropes alongside the other men. Together, they wheeled the cannon into place, blocking off the last escape from Trenton.

Just then, another group of Hessians arrived, trying to escape over the bridge. When they saw that it was already under the control of Washington's army, they filed up the creek, searching for another place to cross. Glover's men fired on them and pushed them into a swampy area, where the Hessian cannons got hopelessly stuck in the mud.

"Again!" a voice boomed. "Fire!" Isaac wasn't sure who'd given the order. The commands and cannon booms pounded in his ears, and his vision grew blurry. He started toward the cannon crew but stumbled and fell. Ranger rushed to his side.

Isaac tried to stand, but his wounded leg buckled under him. He sank to the frozen ground, and everything went black.

Chapter 15

RESCUE IN THE SNOW

Ranger nudged Isaac's cheek with his nose, but Isaac didn't open his eyes. The other men from Glover's regiment had pushed forward, surrounding the Hessians in the swamp. No one seemed to notice that Isaac had fallen.

Ranger sniffed at Isaac's leg. It smelled of dirt and river water and blood. Too much blood. Ranger didn't want to leave, but Isaac needed help.

Ranger ran toward the other men. Just as he reached them, the cannon booms ended, and a different noise rose up from the troops.

Soldiers were shouting and clapping one another's shoulders. Ranger ran up to one of them and pawed at his leg.

The man looked down and shouted, "We've done it, dog! The Hessians surrendered! We've beaten them!"

The man kept celebrating. Ranger needed someone who would pay attention. Where was Joe? Ranger weaved his way through the soldiers, sniffing the air until he caught Joe's scent. He followed it through the men and behind a clump of trees.

There! Ranger ran to Joe and jumped up on him.

"Where've you been, dog?" Joe said. He bent to pat Ranger's head.

Ranger backed away and kept barking.

Joe frowned. "What is it?" Then he looked around. "Where's our friend? Where's Isaac?"

Ranger took a few steps in Isaac's direction. Then he ran back and jumped up on Joe's legs. He barked and raced back and forth until Joe and another soldier followed him back to the spot where Isaac lay in a heap in the snow.

"Isaac!" Joe looked down at Isaac's leg wound. "Bring a cart," he told the other soldier. "He needs a doctor."

The other man ran off. Joe wrapped his blanket around Isaac's blood-soaked thigh. He shook Isaac's shoulder. "Come on, wake up."

Ranger licked Isaac's cheek. His skin was clammy and cold. But his eyelids fluttered open.

"That's it, now," Joe said. "Stay with me. You're hurt, but we've sent for help."

Ranger stayed close at Isaac's side. When the other soldier returned with two more men and a cart, Ranger walked with them to the river. Joe and the other soldiers loaded Isaac into one of the boats. They let Ranger jump in beside him. Ranger sat next to Isaac in the icy, slushy water at the bottom of the boat. It didn't matter that he was cold and wet. All that mattered was Isaac getting help.

On the other side of the river, the soldiers loaded Isaac into another cart, and Ranger trotted alongside it, all the way back to camp. He had to wait outside while a doctor operated on Isaac's leg. It took a long, long time.

Finally, Joe arrived. He lifted the tent's flap and looked inside. Then he turned to Ranger. "Come on, dog." He slapped his leg and held the flap open, and Ranger followed him inside.

Isaac lay on a long table, his leg wrapped in bandages. He wasn't awake.

"How is he, sir?" Joe asked the doctor. "Will he be all right?"

"He should be," the doctor said.

Ranger walked carefully up to Isaac and sniffed at his cheek.

Isaac opened his eyes. "Hello, dog," he whispered. He looked up at the other men. "What happened?"

"You took a musket ball in your thigh," the doctor said.

"What about the battle?" Isaac asked.

The doctor grinned. "It was a victory. And without losing a single man to enemy bullets. General Washington is most grateful."

Isaac looked at Joe. "You'll have quite a story to tell when we get home. You should start by telling me what I missed out there." Isaac tried to sit up, but the doctor put a hand on his shoulder.

"In time, my friend," Joe said. "You need to rest now."

The doctor nodded. "We were lucky to save

your leg. It's good that your friend found you when he did."

"Thanks to the dog," Joe told Isaac. "He's the one who brought me to you."

Isaac reached out and put his hand on Ranger's head. "Thank you, dog," he said. Even back in Trenton, in the chaos of the battle, Isaac had felt the presence of this golden dog at his side.

Ranger leaned into Isaac's hand. In a little while, Joe left, and the doctor went to tend to another patient. The celebration sounds outside began to fade. The camp was hushed.

Then a quiet hum came from a corner of the hospital tent. Ranger knew even before he looked that it was his first aid kit. One of the soldiers must have brought it here. And now it was humming again.

Finally, his work was done. It was time to go home.

Ranger let Isaac stroke his fur a little while longer. But the humming sound was already getting louder. He turned and started to walk away.

"Wait, dog!" Isaac pulled the knotted rope from his jacket and dangled it off the table.

Ranger took the other end in his teeth and gave it a tug. Isaac pulled back and smiled.

"I hope you'll come with us wherever we go next," he said. But somehow, he already felt as if the dog might be leaving. "If you don't, though . . . I want you to have this." He let go of the rope. "Keep it. And remember me."

Isaac leaned back then, and closed his eyes to rest.

Ranger carried the rope in his mouth and found his first aid kid under a pile of blankets in a far corner of the tent. Ranger nuzzled the strap over his head. The humming was much louder now, and the old metal box felt warm at

Ranger's throat. Light was already spilling from the cracks. It grew brighter and brighter. So bright that Ranger had to close his eyes.

When he opened them, he was standing in the mudroom, and Luke was walking through the door.

Chapter 16

MARSHMALLOWS AND MEMORIES

Ranger lowered his head and let the old first aid kit fall onto his dog bed. He pawed at his blanket until it was covered up. Then he dropped the old, frayed rope on top.

"Hey, Ranger!" Luke stood by the door with a bag of marshmallows. "Whatcha doing?" He bent and picked up the rope. "Where's this from?"

Ranger took the end of it in his teeth and tugged.

"You want to play tug-of-war?" Luke pulled back for a while. Then he let go. Carefully,

Ranger nuzzled the old rope under his blanket.

"Okay, I can take a hint," Luke said, laughing. "We don't have to play anymore. But do you want to come outside?"

Ranger trotted up to Luke and licked his marshmallow-sugary hand. Then he sat and waited for an ear scratch. When Luke didn't do that right away, Ranger nudged his hand.

"You need some love, huh?" Luke put down the marshmallows, knelt beside Ranger, and gave him a big hug. "Sorry those fireworks scared you. But they're over now. You should come outside." He went to the door and held it open. "Come on, Ranger . . . let's go."

Ranger sat by his dog bed. He didn't want to go out unless the fireworks were really over. It didn't sound loud out there anymore, but you could never be sure with fireworks. Luke

was going no matter what, though. And he was taking the marshmallows.

Ranger trotted to the door. He was glad to be home, but he'd never forget Isaac. Ranger understood that even though his work was done for now, Isaac still had journeys and battles ahead of him. But somehow, Ranger knew that the brave boy with the strong rowing arms would be all right.

"I'm going out to the fire." Luke was holding the door. "You coming, Ranger?"

Ranger went outside and followed Luke into the yard, over to the firepit, where Dad was adding more wood. The fireworks were over. Only the moon lit the sky. All Ranger could hear were Sadie and Mom laughing and the fire crackling. It smelled good. Like wood smoke and toasted marshmallows and home.

AUTHOR'S NOTE

Isaac Pope is a fictional character, but his story is based on the experiences of real soldiers who served in Colonel John Glover's Fourteenth Continental Regiment. They were called the Marblehead Mariners because nearly all of them had served on fishing boats together, based in the town of Marblehead, Massachusetts. The Fourteenth Continental Regiment included a number of African-American and Native soldiers, and they really did sneak George Washington's army across the East River in the middle of the night to escape from the Redcoats after the Battle of Long Island. In less than nine hours, they ferried almost nine thousand men across the river.

From there, the Marblehead Mariners fought in several more battles in New York and retreated through New Jersey. They arrived at Washington's camp in Pennsylvania just days before he launched the Christmas night raid on Trenton. That effort may well have been impossible without Glover's mariners to man the boats and without the Continental Army spies who supplied Washington with critical information necessary to carry out the attack.

The officer who gives Isaac his spying mission is fictional. But the letter from General Washington was real. In December of 1776, Washington wrote to his officers and asked them to look for men who might be helpful as spies. They were asked to find "some person who can be engaged to cross the river as a spy, that we may, if possible, obtain some knowledge of the enemy's situation, movements, and intention. Particular inquiry should be made by the person sent, if any preparations are making to cross the river; whether any boats are building and where; whether they are coming over land from Brunswick; whether any great collection of horses is made, and for what purpose. Expense must not be spared in procuring such intelligence, and it will readily be paid by me."

Isaac Pope's spy mission was inspired by the stories of real-life spies who worked for the Continental Army. James Armistead was an enslaved man who joined the Continental Army in 1781 and served under the Marquis de Lafayette, the commander of the French forces who had come to help the Continental Army. Armistead posed as a runaway slave who'd been hired by the British to spy on the Americans, and British General Cornwallis welcomed him into his camp. Armistead went back and forth from there to the American forces, relaying information that ultimately helped the Continental Army win the Battle of Yorktown, which ended the war.

Washington reportedly had at least one spy who studied the roads and terrain around Trenton and reported back to him about that and about the number of Hessian troops there. Historians believe this intelligence helped him plan the Christmas night attack.

Interestingly enough, Rall also got important information from spies just before the attack on Trenton. Two brothers who had remained loyal to England, Abraham and Moses Doane, apparently saw Washington's troops preparing for the crossing. They hurried to tell Rall, but he was at a party and refused to be interrupted, so his servants wouldn't let the brothers in. The brothers wrote a note instead, and when the servant delivered it, Rall was busy playing cards and shoved it in his pocket instead of reading it.

When Christmas night arrived, men like Isaac really did man the boats that moved Washington's entire army across the Delaware River, and the weather was every bit as miserable as it's described in this story. John Greenwood, a fifer from Boston, described the brutal weather that night:

"Over the river we then went in a flat-bottomed scow . . . and we had to wait for the rest and so began to pull down fences and make fires to warm ourselves, for the storm was increasing rapidly. After a while it rained, hailed, snowed, and froze, and at the same time blew a perfect hurricane . . ."

Today, the site of the crossing of the Delaware is a state park, with a museum that shares the story of the Fourteenth Continental Regiment's role in the attack on Trenton.

After the crossing was complete, the Battle of Trenton itself only lasted a couple of hours. Washington didn't lose any men to enemy bullets during the battle, though several did die from exposure in that awful weather. Twenty-two Hessians were killed, and many more were taken prisoner.

A famous painting that depicts this historic river crossing hangs in New York City's Metropolitan Museum of Art. But historians are quick to point out that this particular piece is more art than history. It was painted by a German artist named Emanuel Leutze,

SITE OF CROSSING
VIEW OF THE DELAWARE RIVER AT THE SITE WHERE
WASHINGTON CROSSED FROM PENNSYLVANIA TO
NEW JERSEY, CHRISTMAS NIGHT 1776 WITH 2400
MEN. ARTILLERY AND SUPPLIES THE TROOPS
MARCHED NINE MILES TO ATTACK THE HESSIANS
STATIONED AT TRENTON. THE BATTLE OF TRENTON
DECEMBER 2, 1776 RESULTED IN A GREAT VICTORY

more than seventy years after the battle. The Delaware River doesn't look like this at the point where Washington's army crossed. It's likely that Leutze actually painted the Rhine, a river in his homeland, to portray it instead. The boats shown in the painting aren't the Durham boats that were actually used that night. Those were larger, carried forty men, and had higher sides. Finally, given the stormy conditions and swirling ice chunks that came careening down the river, George Washington's noble stance in the painting is quite a stretch as well. If he'd been standing like that on the night of the crossing, he'd almost certainly have toppled right into the icy river. And that flag shown in the boat? It wasn't around yet on the night they crossed the river. That version of the American flag didn't exist until 1777.

Isaac's battle with smallpox was also

based on historic accounts of disease during this time period. In the early days of the American Revolution, far more members of the Continental Army died from diseases than from battle. Smallpox turned out to be more dangerous than the enemy's bullets or bayonets. George Washington had smallpox himself when he was a teenager, so he knew of its horrors and he realized that it was threatening to wipe out his army. Finally, he made the decision to have all his troops inoculated, or given vaccines. In February 1777, Washington wrote, "Finding the Small pox to be spreading much and fearing that no precaution can prevent it from running through the whole of our Army, I have determined that the troops shall be inoculated. This Expedient may be attended with some inconveniences and some disadvantages, but yet I trust in its consequences will have the most happy effects. Necessity not only authorizes but seems to require the measure, for should the disorder infect the Army in the natural way and rage with its usual virulence we should have more to dread from it than from the Sword of the Enemy." Washington's decision was controversial at the time. Many people were still afraid of the vaccine, but ultimately, historians agree that it probably saved his army.

Isaac and Joe are fictional characters, but they were inspired by more than five thousand African-American men, both free and enslaved, who served with the Patriots at some point during the Revolutionary War. These men fought with no promise of freedom, and most of them found themselves enslaved again when the war ended.

Isaac's reflections on George Washington's policy toward black soldiers are based on historical facts. When Washington took command of the Continental Army in 1775, he ordered an end to the recruitment of black soldiers, whether those men were free or enslaved. Those who were already enlisted in the North, many of whom fought bravely at Lexington, Concord, and Bunker Hill, were only allowed to finish their terms of service.

What was behind this racism? Washington was from Virginia, and plantation owners in the South worried that arming African-American men could result in slave uprisings. They feared that more than they feared the British Army.

But Washington's policy didn't last. In 1775, the British Army started actively recruiting enslaved men, promising them freedom as long as they'd run away from Patriots and not Loyalists. Within a month, eight hundred men had joined the unit known as Lord Dunmore's Ethiopian Regiment.

This forced the Continental Army to change its policy. In January 1776, Washington allowed free black men with prior military experience to enlist, and that offer was extended to all free black men in 1777. Soon after, Washington approved a plan for Rhode Island to raise a regiment of free blacks and enslaved men.

What happened to the enslaved people who fought with the British in the Revolutionary War? Many were captured and forced back into slavery after the Battle of Yorktown. Others escaped to New York.

In 1782, American and British officials signed the treaty that granted Americans independence. As part of that deal, Americans demanded the return of their property, including enslaved men who had run away to fight with the British. Britain's officers said no. They created a list of the African-Americans who had served Britain in the war and made arrangements for some of them to be evacuated. Ultimately, three to four thousand African-American people boarded ships in New York and left for Nova Scotia, as well as Britain and Jamaica. Unfortunately, those who ended up in Nova Scotia didn't find a much better living situation there. Many became indentured servants, working under terrible conditions with few rights in a cold place far from home.

As for the enslaved men who fought for the Continental Army, a few were freed when the war ended. Most, however, were still considered property. They were sent back into slavery by the country they'd helped to found, and never tasted the freedom for which they'd fought.

FURTHER READING

If you would like to learn more about the American Revolution, the role of African-American soldiers, Revolutionary spies, smallpox, and working dogs, check out the following books and websites:

BOOKS

Answering the Cry for Freedom: Stories of African Americans and the American Revolution by Gretchen Woelfle, illustrated by R. Gregory Christie (Calkins Creek, 2006)

A Spy Called James: The True Story of James Lafayette, Revolutionary War Double Agent by Anne Rockwell, illustrated by Floyd Cooper (Millbrook Press, 2016)

DK Eyewitness Books: American Revolution by Stuart Murray (DK Children, 2015)

George Washington, Spymaster: How the Americans Outspied the British and Won the Revolutionary War by Thomas B. Allen (National Geographic, 2007)

Sniffer Dogs: How Dogs (and Their Noses) Save the World by Nancy Castaldo (Houghton Mifflin Harcourt, 2014)

WEBSITES

"Crossing of the Delaware." George Washington's Mount Vernon digital encyclopedia. http://www.mountvernon.org /library/digitalhistory/digital-encyclopedia /article/crossing-of-the-delaware/

"Disease in the Revolutionary War." George Washington's Mount Vernon digital encyclopedia. http://www.mountvernon.org /library/digitalhistory/digital-encyclopedia /article/disease-in-the-revolutionary-war/

Washington Crossing Historic Park. https:// www.washingtoncrossingpark.org/#

SOURCES

Alden, John Richard. *General Charles Lee: Traitor or Patriot?* Baton Rouge: Louisiana State University Press, 1951.

Billias, George Athan. *General John Glover and His Marblehead Mariners.* New York: Henry Holt & Company, 1960.

Chernow, Ron. *Washington: A Life.* New York: Penguin Press, 2010.

Daigler, Kenneth A. *Spies, Patriots, and Traitors: American Intelligence in the Revolutionary War.* Washington, D.C.: Georgetown University Press, 2014.

Dobyns, Lloyd. "Fighting . . . Maybe for Freedom, but probably not." Colonial Williamsburg. CW Journal, Autumn 2007, accessed March 10, 2018. http://www.history.org/

foundation/journal/autumn07/slaves
.cfm.

Fenn, Elizabeth A. *Pox Americana: The Great Smallpox Epidemic of 1775–82*. New York: Hill and Wang, 2001.

Fischer, David Hackett. *Washington's Crossing*. Oxford: Oxford University Press, 2004.

Gilbert, Alan. *Black Patriots and Loyalists: Fighting for Emancipation in the War for Independence*. Chicago: The University of Chicago Press, 2012.

Heyrman, Christine Leigh. *Commerce and Culture: The Maritime Communities of Colonial Massachusetts, 1690–1750*. New York: W.W. Norton & Company, 1984.

Ketchum, Richard M. *The Winter Soldiers*. Garden City, NY: Doubleday and Company, 1973.

Markle, Donald E. *The Fox and the Hound:*

The Birth of American Spying. New York: Hippocrene Books, 2014.

McCullough, David. *1776*. New York: Simon & Schuster, 2005.

Misencik, Paul R. *The Original American Spies: Seven Covert Agents of the Revolutionary War*. Jefferson, NC: McFarland & Company, 2014.

Nagy, John. A. *George Washington's Secret Spy War: The Making of America's First Spymaster*. New York: St. Martin's Press, 2016.

National Park Service. "Stories from the Revolution: African Americans in the Revolutionary Period." Accessed March 10, 2018. https://www.nps.gov/revwar/about_the_ revolution/african_americans.html

Rhodehamel, John, H. *The American Revolution: Writings from the War of Independence*. New York: Literary Classics of the United States, 2001.

Schecter, Barnet. *The Battle for New York: The City at the Heart of the American Revolution.* New York: Walker & Company, 2002.

Smith, Samuel Stelle. *The Battle of Trenton.* Monmouth Beach, NJ: Philip Freneau Press, 1965.

ABOUT THE AUTHOR

Kate Messner is the author of *The Seventh Wish*; *All the Answers*; *The Brilliant Fall of Gianna Z.*, recipient of the E. B. White Read Aloud Award for Older Readers; *Capture the Flag*, a Crystal Kite Award winner; *Over and Under the Snow*, a *New York Times* Notable Children's Book; and the Ranger in Time and Marty McGuire chapter book series. A former middle-school English teacher, Kate lives on Lake Champlain with her family and loves reading, walking in the woods, and traveling. Visit her online at katemessner.com.

Ranger has never needed his search-and-rescue training more than when he arrives at the World Trade Center on September 11, 2001. There he meets Risha Scott and her friend Max who have come to work with Risha's mother for a school project. But when the unthinkable happens and the building is evacuated, Risha is separated from her mom. Can Ranger lead Risha to safety and help reunite her family?

Risha Scott held a box of muffins and stared up at the Twin Towers. She loved visiting her mom's office at the World Trade Center. It was fun to walk through the busy, crowded plaza, with its fountain and sculpture and bright flowers. Risha loved the buzz of thousands of people, all going to work in the Twin Towers. Today she and her best friend, Max, got to spend the whole day there! They had to visit a professional workplace as part of their fifth-grade career project. Max's dad worked downtown, too, but his office didn't allow visitors.

"I call that chocolate chip muffin!" Max said as they walked into the lobby with Risha's mom. They waited to sign in at the security desk. Then they'd take the elevators up to the ninety-first floor of the North Tower, where Risha's mother worked.

Risha yawned.

"You're not tired already, are you?" her mom asked, laughing.

"You got me up so early!" Risha said as they waited for the elevator. "But I'm not complaining! Today is going to be amazing." Risha had on her navy blue dress with Mom's pretty green-and-gold scarf tied at her neck. Mom wore the bright purple dress Risha loved, with her cool red-framed glasses and black shoes with little bows on top. Last night, Risha and Mom had even painted their fingernails the same color, a sparkly pale pink. Max was dressed up, too, wearing his dad's favorite red tie.

It was perfect September weather, with a robin-egg-blue sky. On their way to the office, Max and Risha had gone with Mom to vote in the primary election for New York City's mayor. They'd walked another three blocks to pick up muffins for everyone in the office at the fancy bakery Risha loved. Now Risha and Max would get to help Mom at work all day.

"You know what's going to be amazing?" Max tapped a poster on the wall. It was about the Paul Taylor Dance Company's performance in the World Trade Center's outdoor plaza that night. After work, they planned to buy picnic food and stay to watch the show. Risha and Max had taken ballet lessons together when they were younger. Max was still dancing, but Risha had switched to gymnastics in fourth grade.

"That'll be you someday," Risha said, pointing to the men on the poster. She gave Max a fist bump.

"Here we go," Mrs. Scott said as the elevator doors opened. She worked on such a high floor that it took two elevators to get there! When they stepped off the second one, Risha led them down the hall to the office. Mom's company worked with big transport ships to make sure they were following rules and being safe. To be honest, Risha didn't really want to do that kind of work when she got older. She was more interested in being a gymnast and an art teacher. But missing school to spend a whole day downtown with Mom was too great a chance to pass up.

They passed out the muffins, and there were a few left over. Mrs. Scott looked at her watch. "I'm going to take a muffin down to my friend at Port Authority. You can hang out in the conference room, and I'll be right back."

She brought Risha and Max to a big room, at least three times the size of Risha's bedroom. It had a long table with fancy, cushy chairs that spun around. Best of all was the wall of windows that looked out toward the Empire State Building.

"Whoa!" Max said.

Risha smiled. She'd seen the view before and was excited to share it. She pulled her colored pencils and sketchbook out of her backpack. Later, she'd need to take notes for their career project, but for now, she wanted to draw the buildings outside.

"I'll be back in a few minutes. Then I'll introduce you to some people you can interview for your project," Mom said, and closed the conference room door behind her.

"This rocks," Max said. He polished off his muffin in three bites and pulled *Harry Potter and the Goblet of Fire* from his bag.

Risha looked up from her drawing and laughed. "Haven't you already read that like three times?"

"Gets better every time," he said.

Risha went back to work on her drawing. A few minutes later, she heard a sound like an airplane. It got louder and louder. She looked out the window.

A plane was flying low in the sky. Too low! Risha stared as it roared past the Empire State Building.

It was heading straight toward them.

MEET RANGER

A time-traveling golden retriever with search-and-rescue training . . . and a nose for danger!